# Danny's Really Big Show

written and photographed
by
Mia Coulton

Danny was doing card tricks for Bee.

"Now I will do my magic card trick," he said.

"See the cards.

I want you to pick a card, any card.

I won't look and then I will guess what card you picked."

"Is this your card?

I think it is!"

Danny said to Bee.


"Ta-da."

"Next, I will pull a rabbit out of my hat.

Ta-da.

I am going to put on a show, a really big show!

I will do my magic tricks."

Bee got a guitar.

Bee looks like a singer.

Bee wants to sing

in the really big show.

Danny said, "Sing, Bee, sing!"

Bee did not sing.

"Oh, I forgot, you can't sing."

"Come back, Bee!"

Danny shouted.

"Don't leave.

You can do something else

in the really big show."


Bee did not come back.

Bee has left the building.